CINDERELLA

THE DOG AND HER LITTLE GLASS SLIPPER

BY DIANE GOODE

THE BLUE SKY PRESS • AN IMPRINT OF SCHOLASTIC INC. • NEW YORK

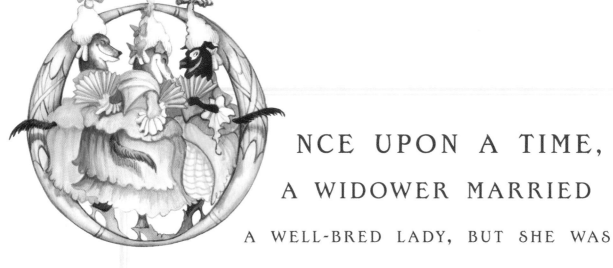

NCE UPON A TIME, A WIDOWER MARRIED A WELL-BRED LADY, BUT SHE WAS thoroughly mean and nasty. Her two daughters were exactly like her. The widower's daughter, however, had a good and noble heart.

No sooner was the wedding over when the new wife began to treat her stepdaughter as a servant. The daughter slept on some old bedding and ate scraps from the table. She never complained to her father, for she knew he had grown afraid of his new wife. When her work was done, she would curl up in the chimney corner among the cinders and ashes. She soon came to be known as Cinderella.

From morning till night, the stepsisters' commands rang through the house.

"Cinderella, polish the pans! Cinderella, clean the grates!

Cinderella, scrub the floors! Cinderella, fetch my supper!"

One day, news came
that a ball was to be given
by the king's son. The stepsisters,
of course, were invited, and began at
once to choose their gowns. On the
day of the ball, Cinderella helped them
dress and arrange their wigs.

"Cinderella," said the younger sister, "don't
you wish you were going to the ball?"

"Oh," said Cinderella, "a great ball is no
place for me."

"Yes indeed!" replied the older sister.
"Everyone would laugh to see such a dirty
dog at the ball."

Now, anyone but Cinderella would have put
the stepsister's wig on backward after that
remark, but Cinderella was so kind, she
combed it perfectly.

When at last the sisters had gone, Cinderella went out into the garden and began to cry.

Suddenly her fairy godmother appeared.

"Do you wish to go to the ball, Cinderella?"

"Yes, yes, I do," said Cinderella.

"Then I shall see to it that you go. First, bring me the largest pumpkin you can find."

Cinderella brought it to her godmother, who tapped it with her wand. It became a splendid golden coach.

"Now, fetch me the mouse trap in the pantry."

Cinderella returned with it, and the godmother opened the wire door. As each mouse scurried out, the godmother tapped it with her wand, and the four mice became horses.

"But what shall we do for a coachman, Cinderella?"

"I saw a plump rat with long whiskers in the rat trap.

He might do."

Cinderella brought the trap, and her godmother transformed

the rat into a fine coachman.

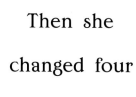

Then she changed four lizards into footmen. They leaped up behind the coach as if they had done it all their lives.

"Are you pleased?" asked the godmother.

"Oh, yes, I am," said Cinderella. "But am I to go to the ball in these dirty rags?"

With a touch of her wand, the godmother turned the rags into a lovely gown. A pair of glass slippers appeared on Cinderella's feet.

"Now, promise that you won't stay a moment past midnight," said the godmother. "If you do, your coach will turn back into a pumpkin, your horses to mice, your coachman to a rat, your footmen to lizards, and your gown to rags."

Cinderella promised.

Cinderella drove through the starlit night to the king's palace.

When she entered the ballroom, the musicians stopped
playing, and all the dancing ceased. Here was a princess
no one had seen before.

The prince made a deep bow and invited Cinderella
to dance. All eyes were upon them.

A great feast was brought in, but the prince could not eat

a bite. All he could do was gaze lovingly at Cinderella. The

king whispered to the queen that he had never seen such a

charming girl.

Cinderella sat down beside her stepsisters, who did not

recognize her, and she offered them the orange that the
prince had given her. Many of the ladies looked closely at her
gown, hoping to have the same dress made for themselves.

Suddenly, the clock struck a quarter to midnight. Cinderella
curtsied to the guests and bounded away as fast as she could.

Safe at home, Cinderella thanked her godmother and asked if she might attend a second ball, for the prince had invited her to come. Just then, Cinderella heard the sisters returning home. She let them in, stretching and yawning as if she had just woken up.

"You've stayed very late!" she exclaimed.

"We could hardly bring ourselves to leave. Everyone was talking about a princess who came tonight. No one knew who she was, and the prince would give anything to find out."

"Is that so?"
murmured Cinderella.
And she smiled.

At the second ball, Cinderella wore a dress even more
lovely than the first. She danced with the prince all night,
and when the clock chimed midnight, she thought it was
only eleven o'clock.

When she realized her mistake, she ran from the ballroom.

The prince chased after her, but all he found was one of her glass slippers.

Panting, and out of breath, Cinderella arrived at home. All that remained of her splendor was the other glass slipper. She hid it in her apron pocket.

When the sisters returned, Cinderella asked if they had seen the mysterious princess again. "Yes, but she ran off when the clock struck midnight, and she lost one of her glass slippers," said the younger. "The prince found it and stared at it all evening," said the elder. "Everyone agrees he has fallen in love with her."

And indeed he had.

The next day, the prince proclaimed that he must find the lady whose foot fit the glass slipper. Princesses, duchesses, and

all the ladies of the court tried it on, but without success. The

slipper had been made by magic, and so it could only be worn

by its true owner.

At last, the slipper was brought to the two stepsisters. They pushed and shoved, but they could not squeeze their toes into it.

"Let me try it on," said Cinderella.

The stepsisters howled with laughter.

But the prince's servant said that his orders were to try it on everyone, so he put the slipper on Cinderella's foot. It fit perfectly. Her stepsisters were amazed. They were even more shocked when she took the other slipper from her pocket.

At that moment,

Cinderella's godmother

appeared. She touched

Cinderella with her wand and changed

her mangy rags into a silken gown.

The stepsisters knew her instantly as

the princess at the ball. They begged her

forgiveness for the cruel way they had treated

her. Cinderella forgave them both, and they

embraced as true sisters.

Then Cinderella was escorted to the palace, where she
told her story to the prince. He found her to be even more
lovable than ever.

Cinderella, who had always understood the wisdom

of kindness, invited her sisters to the wedding to share
in the great celebration.

And she and the prince lived happily, as true and
loyal companions.

FOR PETER

THE BLUE SKY PRESS

Text and illustrations copyright © 2000 by Diane Goode

All rights reserved.

No part of this publication may be reproduced or stored in a retrieval system or

transmitted in any form or by any means, electronic, mechanical, photocopying,

recording, or otherwise, without written permission of the publisher.

For information regarding permission, please write to:

Permissions Department, The Blue Sky Press, an imprint of Scholastic Inc.,

555 Broadway, New York, New York 10012.

The Blue Sky Press is a registered trademark of Scholastic Inc.

Library of Congress catalog card number: 99-086352

ISBN 0-439-07166-6

10 9 8 7 6 5 4 3 2 1   0/0 01 02 03

Printed in Singapore   46

First printing, September 2000

Designed by Kathleen Westray